# The Pig in the Pond

## Martin Waddell

*illustrated by* Jill Barton

CANDLEWICK PRESS
CAMBRIDGE, MASSACHUSETTS

For Charlotte Maeve
*M.W.*

For Porky Boffin
*J.B.*

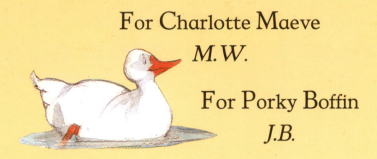

Text copyright © 1992 by Martin Waddell
Illustrations copyright © 1992 by Jill Barton

First U.S. paperback edition 1996

The Library of Congress has cataloged
the hardcover edition as follows:

Waddell, Martin.
The pig in the pond / Martin Waddell ; illustrated by Jill Barton. –1st U.S. ed.
Summary: An overheated pig who doesn't swim, throws himself into a pond,
throwing the farmyard into an uproar.
ISBN 1-56402-050-9 (hardcover)
[1. Pigs–Fiction.  2. Domestic animals–Fiction.]    I. Barton, Jill, ill.  II. Title.
PZ7.W1137Pi   1992
[E]–dc20          91-58751

ISBN 1-56402-604-3 (paperback)

12 14 16 18 20 19 17 15 13 11

Printed in China

This book was typeset in Veronan Light Educational.
The illustrations were done in watercolor and pencil.

Candlewick Press
2067 Massachusetts Avenue
Cambridge, Massachusetts 02140

visit us at www.candlewick.com

This is the story of Neligan's pig.

One day Neligan went into town.
It was hot. It was dry.
The sun shone in the sky.
Neligan's pig sat by
Neligan's pond.

The  ducks went, "Quack!"

The geese went, "Honk!"

They were cool on

the water in

Neligan's pond.

The pig sat in the sun.

She looked at the pond.

The ducks went, "Quack!"

The geese went, "Honk!"

The pig went, "Oink!"

She didn't go in,

because pigs don't swim.

The pig sat in the sun getting hotter and hotter.

The ducks went, "Quack, quack!"     The geese went, "Honk, honk!"

The pig went, "Oink, oink!" She didn't go in, because pigs don't swim.

The pig gulped and gasped and looked at the water.

The ducks went, "Quack, quack, quack!"

The geese went, "Honk, honk, honk!"

The pig went, "Oink, oink, oink!"

She rose from the ground          and turned around          and around,

stamping her feet          and twirling her tail,          and . . .

SPLASH!

SPLASH! SPLASH!

SPLASH! SPLASH!

SPLASH!   SPLASH!

SPLASH!   SPLASH!

The ducks and the geese were splashed out of the pond.

The ducks went, "Quack, quack, quack, quack!"
The geese went, "Honk, honk, honk, honk!"
which means, very loudly, "The pig's in the pond!"

"The pig's in the pond!"        "The pig's in the pond!"

The word spread about, above, and beyond,

"The pig's in the pond!"

"The pig's in the pond!"

"At Neligan's farm, the pig's in the pond!"

From the fields all around they came to see
the pig in the pond at Neligan's farm.
And then . . .

Neligan came on his cart!

Neligan looked at the pig in the pond.

The pig went, "Oink!"

Neligan took off his hat.

Neligan looked at the pig in the pond.

The pig went, "Oink, oink!"

Neligan took off his pants and boots.

Neligan looked at the pig in the pond.

The pig went, "Oink, oink, oink!"

Neligan took off his shirt.

Neligan looked at the pig in the pond.

The pig went, "Oink, oink, oink, OINK!"

Neligan took off his underwear and . . .

**SPLASH**! Neligan joined the pig in the pond.

*fart!*

What happened next?

SPLO

OOOOOOSH!

They all joined the pig in the pond!

And that was the story of Neligan's pig.